THE ADVENTURES OF PETER POCKET AND HIS SKY ROCKET

By Philip Graham

Illustrated by R. V. Mee

BOOK 2

CONTENTS

Introduction

Although Peter Pocket looked like an ordinary boy, he was really rather special. His father had been a wizard and he made Peter a suit with a magic pocket which would provide him with everything he should ever need. This pocket was large and yellow and filled with powder. Each grain of powder was an article which would grow into normal size as soon as it was taken from the pocket. Peter practised until he was able to pick the grain he wanted. It might be a tractor or a boat, indeed anything you could imagine.

As he enjoyed helping people who were in trouble, Peter asked his father to make him something to transport him quickly to places where he could be of use, and so the sky-jet was assembled. It had a trouble detector (T.D. for short), which told Peter when someone was in danger. It also had a T.V. screen to show where the trouble waves were coming from.

Here are just a few of Peter's adventures.

Published by Peter Haddock Ltd.,
Bridlington, England. ©
Printed in Hungary

The Lobster

Have you ever tasted lobster? Many people find it delicious. Dennis and his wife Betty loved them — but they were too expensive to buy regularly and so they had one on special occasions, like birthdays.

Dennis had recently joined a sub-aqua club and had all the gear for underwater swimming. He had trained at the local swimming pool and had twice been with the club when they went to the coast, which was only five miles away.

This had given him the idea of surprising Betty by bringing home a lobster which he had caught himself. He knew she would be delighted and so the plan formed in his mind.

When Betty was shopping, he loaded all his gear in the boot of his car, left her a note saying he'd gone to see some friends and set off for the coast to catch himself a lobster!

He knew a quiet part where no-one went because it was rocky and the little cove had no sand, just a pebble beach. When he got there he changed into his wet suit, put on the heavy air bottle and set off for the water carrying his flippers and a bag — what do you think the bag was for?

He waded into the water, pulled down his goggles and began to swim out to the deeper water.

It was a pleasant day and the sea was calm, so Dennis was enjoying himself. There was only the sound of his own breathing, and the bubbles leaving the outlet valve. Because the sea was calm and the sun was bright, it was very clear that day and Dennis could gaze at the peaceful beauty all round him. The fronds of seaweed waved gently; fish darted in all directions and the large rocks were covered in delicate shades of pink, brown and green.

Ahead of him he noticed the dark shape of an old wreck — a fishing boat which had sunk many years ago. It had never been moved because no boats came near there now, except very small ones used by fishermen.

Dennis swam round and above the wreck. As he peered down he was pleased to see something move. It was a bluey black creature and he saw it scuttle away under a part of the wreck. Dennis was delighted — it was a big lobster!

He swam down to where it had disappeared.

He flattened himself onto the rock and peered into the gloom under the wreck. When his eyes grew accustomed to the darker water, he could see the lobster. He reached out and wriggled under an old piece of chain to get nearer.

He reached out and grabbed the creature round the body. He was about to pull himself out from under the chain when, to his alarm, he found that he was stuck. The valve on his air bottle had somehow got caught up in the old chain and, try as he might, he could not get himself free, he couldn't even get out of the harness which held the bottle, because he couldn't get his hands back to release it.

He was now getting very frightened. It had all gone wrong! Why had he been so silly as to do this alone? He had been told never to dive alone — always with at least one other diver, just in case. He was now breathing heavily with the recent exertions. This meant he was using up his air at a faster rate. He reckoned he had about ten minutes supply left. The sea-bed was a lonely place now — he lay there breathing heavily and feeling very scared.

Ten miles or so down the coast Peter Pocket was cruising in his Sky Rocket and was just

about to head off inland when the T.D. flashed to indicate it was picking up distress waves. Peter flicked some switches which turned on the T.V. and gave a location for the source of the waves.

Up on the screen came the cove and the open sea. Peter turned the Rocket and put it on full thrust. He felt himself being pushed back in his seat as the ship zoomed along on full power. Soon he was circling the cove, and when he saw the car, he landed nearby. The distress waves were coming from the sea and Peter realised that since he could see no-one in the water, the trouble must be below the surface.

Peter wasted no time. He felt in his Magic Pocket for the grains he needed. He let several of them fall on the pebbles and instantly they changed into the equipment he needed – an inflatable boat with an outboard motor; a wet suit and breathing apparatus. He changed quickly into underwater gear; dragged the dinghy to the water, started up the motor and roared out in the direction of the trouble. He cut the engine when he figured he was near the spot and then got himself prepared and slipped over the side of the boat.

9

He swam round in the clear water and searched around until, when he got to the wreck, he spotted a pair of legs sticking out from under the old chain. Was he in time? He swam down and tapped the man on the legs. It made Dennis jump — but he was so relieved when he realised someone had found him. Peter swam round to the front from where he was able to see Dennis and gave him a thumbs up sign to let him know that he'd soon have him out of there. However, when Peter tried to lift the chain and the old piece of steel plate, he could not budge them. He swam back to the dinghy and felt in his Magic Pocket for another grain. When he dropped it in the boat it changed into . . . a car jack.

Back over the side he went and when he reached the wreck he placed the jack under the chain and began to turn the handle. It was hard work, but slowly the chain and the old plate began to inch slowly upwards. Peter made a few more turns then managed to get the valve free. He pulled Dennis by the feet and soon had him out. They smiled at each other and Peter helped Dennis to swim to the surface. They climbed into the dinghy and were soon back on the pebble beach.

Dennis had fully recovered by now and after thanking Peter he vowed never to dive alone again. If it hadn't been for Peter Pocket, the lobsters might have had him for dinner — and when he thought of that it made his face go like a lobster — a boiled one.

Picnic on the River

The children were told not to make any plans for the following Saturday. Dad had said he had a surprise for them all and refused to give any clues. Even Mum just smiled and shrugged her shoulders when they asked her excitedly what was planned.

They chattered eagerly about what it could be. Paul suggested they guess, and said it might be a visit to the city. Emma said there might be a fair coming to their town, maybe that would be the surprise.

At last Saturday came round. The children didn't take long to find out the first part of the plan. The kitchen was filled with food of all kinds and it became obvious that they were off on a picnic — but where?

13

Dad just grinned at all their questions but still kept it a mystery. Soon they were in the car and off for a day out with every sign a good one — the sky was blue, the sun was shining and the air was fresh and warm.

When Dad turned off the main road and drove down the lane past the old mill, they knew it was to be the river — a picnic by the river. But Dad said this was only *nearly* correct, it was not exactly *by* the river, but they were getting warm. What could he mean?

Soon the car was crunching down a gravel drive that gave the children the final answer — it led to the boatyard, and when Emma shouted that they were going for a boat-trip, Dad said that, at last, they had guessed it all. He had hired a small cabin cruiser for the afternoon so that they could have a picnic, not *by* the river but actually *on* the river!

The children were so excited — they buzzed with it. They followed their Dad, who carried the main hamper, up to the little office and listened eagerly as the man in charge said he'd take them to the boat and show them the controls and tell them where they were allowed to go.

They listened as the man told them they could go almost as far as they liked *upstream*, but only as far as the danger buoys *downstream*, because of the weir. Emma asked Paul, in a whisper out of the side of her mouth, what a weir was. He whispered back that it was what they called the waterfall.

They couldn't wait to be off. They loaded all the stuff and sat watching as Dad pressed a button and the engine chugged into life. They waved at the man and started upstream. They gazed over into the clear water and saw the pebbles which seemed to sway in the water below them. They saw little fish darting in all directions and they trailed their hands in the clear water as the little boat made its way against the gentle flow of the river.

The next two hours were pure delight. They chugged on past fields and woods and kept pointing excitedly at all the wonders they saw. Paul noticed a large pike lying motionless among the reeds with its menacing mouth ready to snatch at any poor fish that came near. Emma spotted a beautiful blue-coloured bird that flashed past them and Mum told them it was a kingfisher.

On they went, seeing rabbits and pheasants; weeping willows at the edge of the river and all sorts of lovely wild flowers growing on the banks.

At last, Dad spotted a pretty place to stop, and asked if anyone was hungry — what do you think? They sat round the hamper and were soon tucking into salmon sandwiches, cakes, sausage rolls and pieces of cold chicken. Flasks and bottles were opened so that they could have coffee or orange or coke to finish.

When they had finished their meal, they had another enjoyable trip back down to the boatyard. Paul and Emma were even given a turn at the wheel. Steering was great fun, and they soon learned how to do it.

Dad looked at his watch when they neared the boatyard. He suggested that as they still had more than an hour of their time left, they might as well go downstream for a short trip before driving home.

The river below the yard grew much wider and soon they could see, ahead of them, the two red buoys which marked the limit for all boats. To go further than this was dangerous because, a few hundred yards further down, was the weir

where the water tumbled over in a six foot waterfall which they could hear as a faint rumble even at that distance.

They were right out in the middle when something happened which caused them to look at each other in alarm. The engine stopped. It just spluttered and then all was silent. Dad pressed the starter again and again but all it did was splutter feebly — it would not start.

The current was fast down here and the little boat was now gliding down quite quickly. Without power they could not turn back, what should they do?

The noise of the weir grew louder and Dad knew they were in trouble. He had tried to head for the bank but the river had just taken them on. Ahead of them he noticed part of an old dead tree sticking up from the water — it had probably been swept down during the floods the previous winter. As they neared it Dad told everyone to try and grab one of the branches. As it came up alongside them they all reached out. Paul remembered there was a boat hook, on a long pole, in the bottom of the boat. Quickly he picked it up and reached out for the tree. After two or three attempts, he managed to hook one

of the stronger branches. Dad saw this and went to help Paul. They both pulled with all their might and slowly they inched towards the tree so that Mum and Emma could also hold on to the branches.

They felt the tug of the current pulling hard against them. They held on tightly, but how long could they fight against the river? — if they let go they would be swept down and over the falls into the raging waters below — and in there they wouldn't stand a chance.

Could anyone help them? Well, it so happened that Peter Pocket was patrolling about ten miles away. As he sped along in his Sky Rocket, he picked up the distress waves on his T.D. He located the source and turned his ship in that direction. He took her up to full power and roared across the sky towards the family who were still holding on grimly, even though their arms ached and they felt very afraid.

Peter was soon over the scene and could see the plight of the people in their boat. He zoomed in and made a hover-landing on the bank.

They were about thirty yards out from him and he could tell from the pained looks on their

tired faces, that they could not hold on for much longer.

Peter felt in his Magic Pocket and took out three grains. When he dropped them they turned immediately into, a ball of string, a rope and a crossbow. The crossbow had a bolt all ready for firing. Peter tied the string to the bolt and aimed at the side of the boat. He pulled the trigger and the bolt flashed across the water, through the branches of the old tree, and made a hollow thud as it stuck into the wooden side of the cabin cruiser.

They could see what Peter was planning. Paul grabbed the twine and pulled the rope which Peter had now tied to the other end.

Soon, Paul had pulled the rope over and tied it to the front of the boat. Peter tied his end to a tree on the river bank. For the time being, they were safe, but now they had to be rescued.

Peter took out another magic grain. This time it turned into a powerful blue jet-boat. He pushed it into the water, jumped aboard and started the engine. He drove over and carefully came alongside the cruiser.

Seconds later they were all skimming over the water heading for the boathouse.

Peter joined the family for tea that evening and they all chatted about the narrow escape — in a way, that is what they'd had — an *arrow* escape.

Mayday! Mayday!

Mayday is the signal sent out when someone is in trouble. It comes from the French words which mean "Help me!" People send out this message over their radios if their ship or plane gets into danger.

One day, as Peter flew his Sky Rocket a few miles from a small airport, he picked up a Mayday call on his radio.

It came from a light aircraft which had been about to land when the pilot found that his front wheel was stuck. He was now circling the airport and warning them that he would have to make a crash landing without using the wheels.

Peter heard him ask for fire engines and ambulances to be standing by when he made his landing — this could be very dangerous indeed. As Peter listened in and watched the plane prepare for its approach, a plan was forming in his

mind. He thought he knew of a way to bring the plane in more safely.

He had to act quickly, so he got into radio contact with the pilot and told him what he planned to do. By now they could see each other and the pilot agreed to try Peter's plan and gave him a thumbs up sign as Peter flew alongside.

Peter knew how to handle the Sky Rocket and now he had a chance to show just how skilful he was!

Carefully, he brought the powerful little rocket-ship underneath the plane. Then he inched forward until he was directly below the faulty front wheel — as he looked up he could see it lying flat in its housing near the nose.

Peter now edged closer underneath the plane until he felt a slight jolt as the two crafts touched.

It was now up to Peter and the pilot to keep their machines in contact whilst they made an attempt to land. They made a large circle and then headed for the runway in a very gradual descent.

The runway came nearer and nearer. Soon it was racing below them as the two crafts began to throttle-back for the touchdown. The wheels

of the plane and the Sky Rocket touched at almost the same moment, and everyone held their breath and hoped that the little rocket ship could support the nose of the plane until it had slowed to a safe speed.

Peter could hear a creaking noise as the rocket began to take the weight of the plane — would it hold? Yes, the little rocket was strongly built and the nose of the plane stayed in place until the last few yards when it slowly slid down. But it did not matter for now — they were safe!

When they got out, the pilot and his two passengers made a big fuss of Peter and took him to the airport restaurant where they all had a celebration meal.

The pilot thanked Peter again and finished by saying that this was one time when he hadn't minded being "held-up" during a flight.

Quicksand

Peter was enjoying a fine view of the estuary as he circled in his Sky Rocket. The sun was glinting on the calm blue sea whilst flocks of seabirds were busy feeding at the water's edge. Far

below him, Peter could see a lone motor-cyclist enjoying the freedom of the vast empty beach. Peter watched as he raced over the sand dunes and then sped down towards the sea — he was having the time of his life roaring around making circular patterns in the sand.

The scene below was so peaceful that Peter was startled when the T.D. began to flash. What could it be? He switched on the small screen and then the mystery was solved. It was the motor-cyclist who was in trouble. He had stopped near some rocks on a very wet patch. His engine was still racing and the back wheel was sending a stream of mud into the air as it whizzed round. But then Peter could see that the front wheel, and the man's feet had sunk deep into the oozey mud — it was quicksand, and he was sinking into it!

Peter summed up the situation and headed for a patch of dry sand a few yards from the man. By now, the front wheel had nearly disappeared and the man was up to his thighs when he spotted Peter and cried for help.

Peter felt in his Magic Pocket and pulled out two grains. When exposed to the air the grains quickly changed into a long coil of strong rope

and a machine which looked like a small engine on wheels. This machine was an air-pump called a compressor.

Firstly, Peter threw the rope to the man and told him to tie it around his chest and under his arms. As the man was doing this Peter tied the other end to a tree nearby, and so prevented the man from sinking any further.

There was now, however, another menace to add to the problem — the tide was coming in rapidly! Already the man and his bike were not only stuck fast but were also in six inches of water.

It would have been useless to try to pull the man out for the quicksand holds you like a vice. Peter knew this and that was why he had picked a grain which had changed into a compressor. This was the latest invention for releasing people trapped in mud and quicksand.

There was no time to lose! Peter switched on the compressor and paddled out as close to the man as he dared — treading carefully and testing the sand under his feet. When he was near enough, he stuck the end of the hose nozzle into the sand around the trapped man. It made a fizzing noise as millions of tiny air bubbles

frothed around in the sand. The water was now a foot deep and the man looked very frightened.

Gradually, as the air bubbles loosened the deadly grip of the sand, the man was able to move his legs. He pulled at the rope and pressed his foot against the bike to give him some leverage — as Peter pulled with all his might.

Slowly but surely, Peter pulled the man clear of the bike and out of the water.

Only the top of the back wheel was visible as the man lay staring at it. Peter gave him a drink from his flask.

The man had lost his bike but had nearly lost something much more precious. He had also learned that the coast can be dangerous — even on a lovely sunny day.

The Gold Necklace

Julie was so happy. It was her birthday, and, among all her other presents, she had been given one which she prized above all the others — her mother's gold charm necklace. It was made of a fine gold chain from which hung five

gold lucky charms − a star; a diamond; a heart; a clover leaf and a tiny golden rabbit.

She looked at it in the mirror and asked her mother if it would be alright to wear it for the picnic party that afternoon. Her mother had said that would be a lovely idea for it went beautifully with her new party dress.

The beach party was a lovely affair. Her parents and friends had enjoyed themselves in a place on the dunes which they had entirely to themselves. After a glorious day of swimming, sunbathing and playing ball, Julie was pleasantly tired as she lay back in the car seat as her Dad drove them all back home.

When all her friends had gone home, Julie kissed her Mum and Dad and thanked them for a lovely birthday. She said she was going to change into her jeans and go for a ride on her bike before bedtime.

As she was changing she suddenly felt an awful feeling and in just one second, this lovely day was completely ruined . . . can you guess why?

She sat on the bed and her eyes filled with tears as she realised what had happened. The necklace was no longer around her neck! She felt so unhappy and bewildered that it was quite

a few minutes before her poor brain could think straight. Then she decided that she must go and search for it because it would break her heart to have to tell her mother the awful truth.

She dried her eyes and went downstairs; took her bike from the garage and set off for the beach road. She arrived at the picnic spot and straightaway began to search frantically for the necklace. However, after five minutes of sifting through the fine dry sand she felt her eyes well-up with fresh tears as she realised how hopeless it all was.

At this very moment, who do you think was flying around that area? That's right — Peter Pocket was on a routine patrol and it wasn't long before the T.D. picked up the distress waves which were coming from Julie.

Peter landed nearby and went over to Julie and asked her what was wrong. She sobbed out the whole sad story of the necklace and how she could not face the task of telling her mother because it would make her so unhappy.

Peter said that he would like to try to find the necklace, but he said that, before they begin to search, she must think very carefully about the last time she remembered seeing it.

She thought hard and then remembered that she had taken it off to go swimming and had then put it back on just before playing with a beach ball with her friends. They found the place where they had played ball and Peter reached into his Magic Pocket and felt for a grain he wanted. He took it out and dropped it on the sand. Immediately, it changed into just what they needed — an electronic metal detector complete with earphones.

Peter decided to mark the area in strips and, as Julie helped to do this, he began to pace out slowly along the first strip — listening intently in the earphones for the high pitched tone which would signal the presence of metal.

Just near the end of the second strip, Peter signalled excitedly to Julie that he'd found a metal object. Julie dug with her hands and what do you think she found . . . a rusty old sardine tin.

There were three more false alarms as they unearthed a small coin, another tin and a very old bent spoon. Poor Julie, she was almost on the verge of tears when once more Peter signalled that he'd found metal. Julie dug down and, even before she saw the object, her fingers

told her the wonderful news. Slowly she pulled the object from the fine sand and there before her, glinting in the evening sun, was a tiny gold rabbit.

She hugged the necklace to herself and then thanked Peter for his kind help. She insisted on Peter coming back home with her, and staying to supper – after all there was plenty of food still left from the party. So, as Peter enjoyed a dish of trifle and cream, Julie told her parents the whole story. When she finished, her Dad said that Peter must have a "magnetic personality" – and they all laughed.

The Big Red Kite

One day, as Peter walked along a cliff path, he stopped to watch a little boy flying a big red kite. The strong breeze lifted the kite up and up and into the clear blue sky.

The boy was having so much fun, as he made the kite do all sorts of tricks by pulling the strings, that he did not seem to realise he was moving nearer and nearer to the edge of the cliff.

Before Peter could shout to warn him, the boy reached the very edge. He gave a cry as he felt himself fall, and then he was gone!

Peter rushed over and crawled to the spot. He looked over and saw the boy clinging to a bush that grew from a narrow ledge. If Peter did not act quickly, the boy would fall to the rocks below.

Peter felt in his Magic Pocket for a rope grain. He threw it down on the ground and in an instant it grew to a large coil of strong white rope. He tied a loop in one end and lowered it down towards the boy. The boy soon had the rope around his chest and was ready to be pulled up.

Slowly Peter pulled the rope until the boy was safe at the top. Peter then told him to follow and ran down the steps that led to the beach, for Peter was not content simply to rescue the boy — he wanted to rescue something else as well. (Can you guess what it was?) That's right, the kite had fallen into the sea and was now bobbing up and down a short distance from the beach.

Peter reached in his pocket and took out a grain which he dropped near the water's edge. Instantly, it became a shiny blue motor-boat!

They got in and were soon zipping over the waves towards the kite. The boy leaned over and pulled the kite from the water. It was not damaged, and when the strings had been untangled, it was as good as new.